MW00901904

The Gretchen Beckner Story

BY KEVIN POWELL

Dedication:
To my Mom & Dad, my sister Caitlin,
and Snowman!

Acknowledgement:
Special thanks to Steve Stinson and
Olivia Almanza

Copyright © 2020, Kevin Powell

About the Author:

Kevin Powell is a young adult on the autism spectrum, who channels his creative energy writing stories and plays.

He creates superheroes like Gretchen Beckner to help sort out the emotions of daily living and manage the everyday challenges of growing up.

From early childhood, he has enjoyed a lasting friendship with his always smiling Snowman.

Together they have starred in many home movies and captured the hearts of family and friends.

She was getting ready for school, thinking about how this year would be different.

PART ONE

Bullies

ALL her life Gretchen Beckner was picked on by people, doing things like teasing, hitting, and kicking her and even giving her wedgies and stuff. She hoped this year would be different since she was in high school. She was getting ready for school, thinking about how this year would be different. She was ready to go and grabbed her backpack, got on the bus and found her seat.

As she walked to her seat, she noticed a girl holding an upside-down bottle - suddenly she slipped in a puddle of water and fell in the aisle. Everyone was laughing at her! She quickly got up and sat in her seat with her head down. She couldn't believe it was happening again! Thankfully, no one on the bus bothered her anymore.

When she got to school, she opened her locker and a pile of water balloons came falling out, drenching her whole body. Two of the girls from the bus looked at her and laughed. She hurried to the restroom to change clothes and didn't notice that they followed her into the room. When she came out of the stall, the girls came up behind her, pushed her down and gave her a wedgie. They said next time it will be a lot worse. She broke free and ran home and thought hard about a way to stop the bullying.

Most Embarrassing Moment

THAT evening, Gretchen thought she had it figured out. She would keep a close eye on everyone, so no one could catch her off guard. The next morning, she got ready and rode her bike instead of taking the bus.

She got to school and headed to her first class. She didn't see anyone and had an uneventful day. That is, until the end of last block. She was heading to her locker, but before she got there, someone jumped out and sprayed a can of soda on her! She yelled, and her face turned bright red! All the kids laughed at her.

She ran away and thought "I need to change my clothes and come up with a better plan." She headed home, and this time decided to do some research on the internet on how to stop from being bullied.

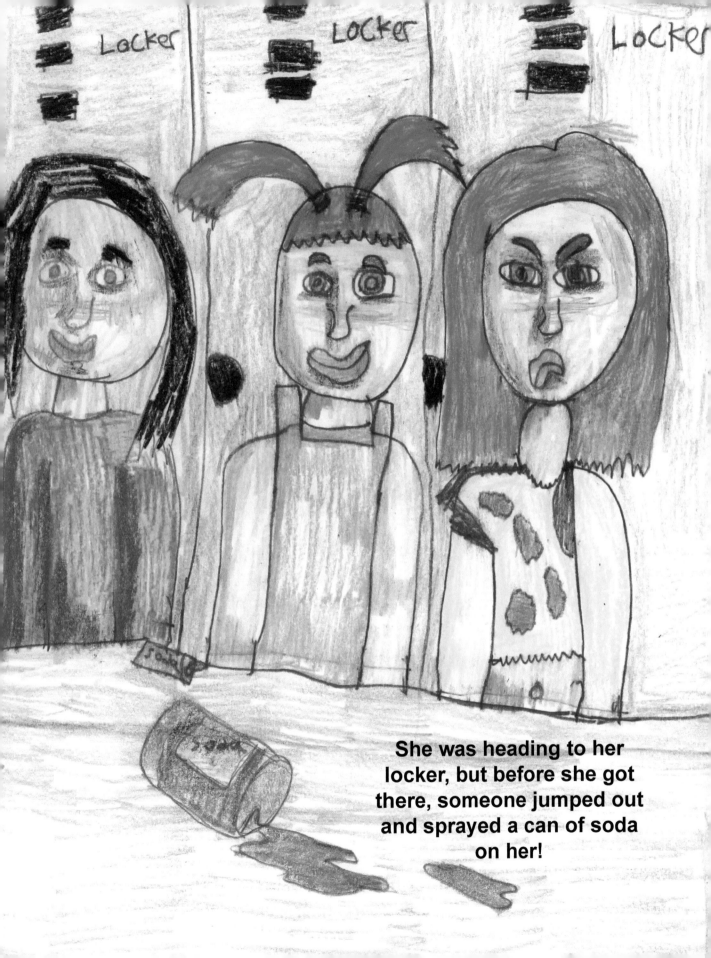

The cop says, "Hands behind your back, both of you!"

Vicious Circle

GRETCHEN was on the computer and made a decision- she was going to try to fight the two girls.

So, the next morning she got ready for school and headed outside to get her bike. As soon as she got outside, she noticed the two girls in the yard. They surrounded her and started calling her names and laughing, then hitting at her and tripping her.

Gretchen yelled and told them to stop and said, "You guys are busted because here comes a cop!"
The cop says "WHAT ARE YOU DOING? STOP THAT"
The girls said, "You're not the boss of us!"
The cop says, "Hands behind your back, both of you!"

The girls ran away, and the cop followed them. Another cop comes out from behind a tree and stuns the two girls and they fall to the ground. The police helped Gretchen up and told her "you're safe, and now these two girls are going to jail"!

Gretchen thanked the police for their help and they said "No problem. We hope you will continue to be a good person, even though bad things have happened to you. We'll see you around."

Gretchen went back to her house and came up with another plan. She decided to become a superhero, so she can help other people who get bullied. She started thinking about what her name will be and what her costume will look like.

Gretchen's First Assignment: Taylor Stevens

GRETCHEN is painting her weapons when she hears a shout.

"Help!"
Gretchen jumped on her motorcycle and went to the bank to see who yelled 'help!
She gets there and saw someone robbing a bank!
"Stop doing this or I will stop you!"
"No!" said the robber.
Gretchen kicks the robber and the cops arrive and put him in handcuffs to take to jail. One of the cops stops to talk to Gretchen.
"Thanks for the help. Can you help us find a bad guy named Taylor Stevens?"

"Yes, but try not to come in 'til I fight her and weaken her," said Gretchen.

"Ok," he replied

Gretchen sees a tall, weird looking tower and goes inside. She sees a camera and thinks, "I need to turn this off." (camera fried)

Suddenly, a laser appears. She dodges the laser and sees Taylor Stevens.
"So, you found me," said Taylor.
"Yea, and you're coming with me!" replied Gretchen

Taylor kicks Gretchen into the laser and runs off.
Gretchen makes it out alive because she stabbed herself with her arrow, which healed her. That's better, she thought.

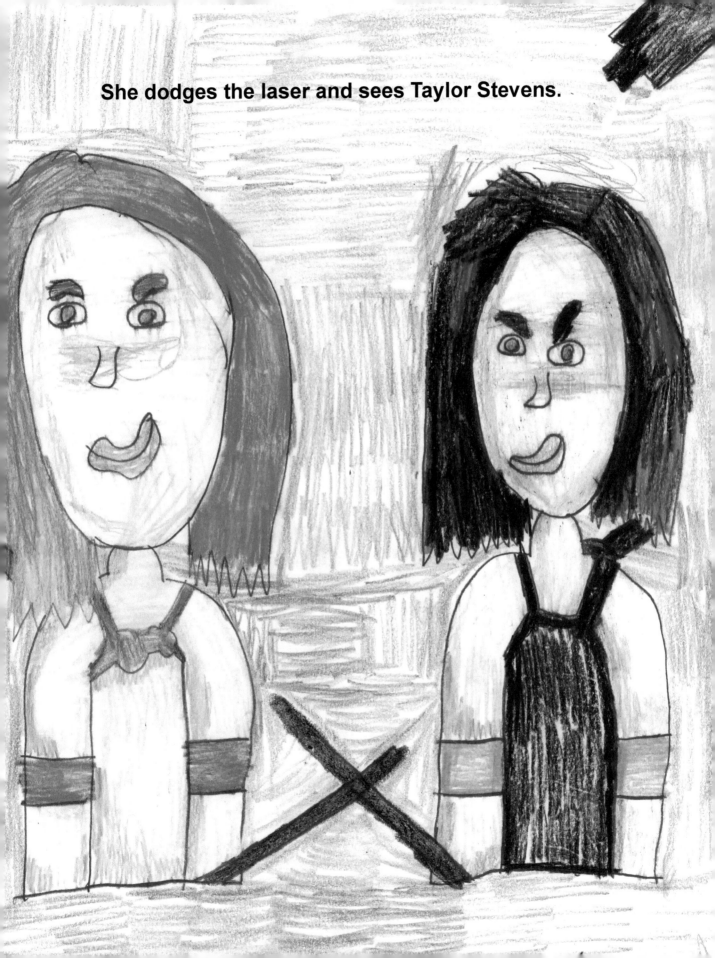

She dodges the laser and sees Taylor Stevens.

When they get there they see a girl tied to a bomb.

Gretchen went to her friend's Kevin's house. She thinks that he can help her find Taylor Stevens.

Kevin and Gretchen look on the computer to see where Taylor will strike next.

"Kevin, let's go save that person!" said Gretchen
"Yes, let's go!"

Gretchen drives to a park and Kevin follows using his flying jet boots. When they get there they see a girl tied to a bomb and Taylor Stevens.

"So, Gretchen, you made it out, good job!"
"Kaitlin, no!" "I will get the bomb, you get Taylor."
"Ok"

Gretchen tried to shoot Taylor with 2 stun pistols, but Taylor jumps out of the way and breaks Gretchen's pistols.

"Well, then eat my arrow, Taylor!"
Gretchen shoots all of her arrows but Taylor dodged all of them.

Next, Gretchen took out her red glasses and nunchucks, but Taylor was too fast and she kicked them out of Gretchen's hands.
"Why do you have glasses as a weapon?"
"If I have them on, I can read your every move."
"I see."

Before things could get any worse the cops show up and handcuff Taylor.

"That was hard, but I did it. Now, to go help Kevin."
"Yep, we've got Taylor from here," said the police.

Kevin stopped the bomb and saved Kaitlin. Then the three of them went back home to rest. Gretchen remade her weapons that were destroyed in battle.

An Attack on the President

MEANWHILE, a guy named Scott is attacking the President.

"Freeze! I want your army to destroy Kevin's Team, so I can be President."
"Ok, do not shoot!"

Scott said to his men, "Go find Kevin's Team." They went to go find the Team.

They saw a girl coming out of a building.

"Who are you? Are you a part of Kevin's Team?"
"Yes, my name is Emily."
"Well, you're coming with us!"

Emily refused so they started shooting at her, but she blocked all the bullets with her sword. Meanwhile, a cop shows up at Kevin's house.

"Kevin, Emily is fighting the army men!"
"Kaitlin, Gretchen, and I are on our way!"
The three of them join to help Emily and they defeat all the men.

Suddenly, they heard a beeping noise. Gretchen goes to check it out and sees that it is Scott on a voice recorder. "You beat my men good. Meet me at the old base. Good bye."

"Ok"

Kevin says, "Emily and Kaitlin, you stay here. Gretchen and I will go find him!"
At the old base, Kevin and Gretchen run into Scott.

"You made it. Nice glasses, Gretchen, but they can't save you now!"

Scott shoots a gun at Gretchen, but reads where he was going to shoot and dodged it. Gretchen shoots her arrow and it hits Scott's leg, making him fall down.

"Run!" shouted Kevin. "No, you will not win, you must suffer" Scott blows himself up.

Kevin and Gretchen hid under a shield to avoid the explosion and then they both go home to rest.

Dominator and Rob Gak

DAVID was driving home from work when he ran over a mine. He jumped out of his car and saw his worst enemies, Dominator and Rob Gak.

"You will not win this fight, Dominator!" shouted David
"We'll see… get him Rob Gak!"

David runs up to Dominator and tries to punch him, but Dominator freezes time and punches David and brings him to his base.

Meanwhile, Gretchen and Kevin hear that David was kidnapped so they try to find him. On the way, they find the base and go inside.

Inside, Dominator and Rob Gak were standing near David, waiting for Gretchen and Kevin to make their move.

"Kevin, do not rush in. My glasses are telling me do not look into Dominator's eyes and keep away from him."

"If you look into my eyes you will die because of too much pressure."
"Why?"
"What!"
"Yea, he is right."

Gretchen shot an arrow but Dominator freezes time and runs to Gretch-

David was driving home from work when he ran over a mine.

She got out a remote control device and pressed a button.

en. But, a second arrow hits Dominator and both Rob Gak and Dominator blow up!

Gretchen saves David, and she and Kevin drop David off at his cabin and they go home to play games.

Suddenly, it started snowing outside - in the middle of summer!

Gretchen went outside to see what was going on and she sees an ice snowman.

"Hello Gretchen. I will freeze the world because I love snow!"

"You can't, the world would die if you make it snow every day!"

"I know."

Gretchen tries to read his moves with her glasses, but it was so cold her glasses froze up. Then Snowman, aka Steven Hearts, punched her.

Gretchen got up and got her swords out. Then, out of nowhere, Taylor Stevens shows up. She broke out of jail to save Gretchen because she was tired of being bad and of Steven Hearts.

So, she got out a remote control device and pressed a button and blew herself up along with Steven Hearts. Luckily, Gretchen hid behind a shield, so she was safe.

All the snow melted and the world was safe again. Gretchen went home to hang out with Kevin.

PART TWO

Eliminator Learns the Truth

HE'S ALIVE!

The Eliminator was at his cousin Dominator's base.

"Dominator, you tried to fight Gretchen Beckner and failed. I will have to be the one to get rid of her."

He heads out to go build the world's biggest bomb to blow up the world! Meanwhile, Gretchen Beckner was getting ready to head out on her motorcycle.

Kevin says, "Are you sure you want to go find Black Heart Snowman?" "Yes," she says. "We need to figure out who is behind all these bad guys who keep coming to fight us.

I'm sure its Black Heart Snowman because every time a bad guy comes, right after the police take them to jail or they die, they always say Black Heart Snowman will finish you."

"Good point," Kevin says.

A cop shows up and says, "Gretchen and Kevin, I'm getting a reading that a big bomb is set to go off. If it does, it will affect the whole world!"

Kevin and Gretchen say, "WHAT??! WE NEED STOP THE BOMB!!!"

He heads out to go build the world's biggest bomb to blow up
the world!

They race to the bomb and when they get there, they see the Eliminator!!
"Who are you?", asks Gretchen.

"My name is the Eliminator, Dominator's cousin," he says, "And for killing him I will kill you and this world that you love so much!!"

"I will not let you blow up this world, I will stop you!!" said Kevin.

Eliminator says, "Very well, let's begin the fight."

Kevin says, "Gretchen, I will get the bomb you take care of the rest!!"
"Got it," says Gretchen.

Kevin tries to hack the bomb and Gretchen swings her sword at Eliminator, but he blocks it with his hand.

"I'm not human, I can stop a sword with my hands" said Eliminator as he breaks one of Gretchen's swords.

"But how???," Gretchen says.
"I'm part robot!", he says, as he runs up and kicks Gretchen to the ground. Then he grabs her neck and starts choking her.

"Stop! I'm sorry for killing Dominator, I didn't mean to!!," said Gretchen.

"It's too late," he says. "it's too late for sorry Gretchen, it's time to die!"

He tries to slice a sword through Gretchen, but she reads the move with her glasses and jumps through Eliminator's legs, going behind him. She puts him in a submission hold.

"The truth is, I did not kill Dominator," said Gretchen. "When I shot the arrow at him, it was actually two arrows. The second one was so close to the first one it looked like I was shooting one, but it was two. The first one blew up Rob, the second one hit Dominator in the leg so the police could take him to jail. So, I did not kill him, just Rob the Robot."

Eliminator said, "What? My cousin is alive?"

"Yes," Gretchen says. "Now how do we stop this bomb?"

"I will stop the bomb," said Eliminator. "if I die, tell Dominator I love him."
"You won't die, I won't let you," said Gretchen.

Kevin stops work on the bomb and lets the Eliminator take over. He hits the blue wire and the green wire and lastly, the pink wire. The bomb stops, and a cop shows up and says "Freeze!"

Kevin says, "Don't shoot, he is with us!'
"Okay," says the cop.
"I want to see Dominator," said Eliminator.
"Ok," said the cop, "We will take you to see him."

He takes the Eliminator to see Dominator and Kevin takes Gretchen to remake her weapons. Then they go home to relax and the Eliminator is finally with Dominator.
Really crazy guy!

He crushed all the bullets with his hands.

BLACK HEART SNOWMAN

MEANWHILE, Black Heart Snowman was working on wiring a minion. Black Heart poured snow into a cup that was connected to the minion. The snow accidentally went down the wire, and the machine overheated.

Black Heart bumped his arm into some nuclear waste, which fell into the cup and went down the wire into the minion's blood and veins. Black Heart jumped out the window and ran to his other base. As Black Heart Minion's body started shaking, the machine he was in blew up and the minion fell on the ground.

Meanwhile, Gretchen was talking to Kevin's friend Will.
"I feel like we are at war," she said.
"I don't think we are at war, you're worrying too much," said Will.
"I hope you're right," she said.
"I am right," he said.

Back at Black Heart's base, Black Heart Minion slowly got up. "I'm alive?" he thought.

The police came in the door and started shooting at the minion. He crushed all the bullets with his hands, and then waved his hands and the cops fell to the ground. The minion says, "You may call me Wedgie Man now. I'm going to make everyone my slave by mind controlling every person in the world."

Wedgie Man left to go to Richmond.

WEDGIE MAN

IN Richmond, Taylor and Jacob were playing Xbox One when the door-bell rang. They didn't answer the door right away, and suddenly the door gets kicked down. Taylor and Jacob hide and try to quietly call Gretchen Beckner.

Wedgie man says, "You can't hide from me forever-you will work for me!!"
Wedgie Man looks through the door with x-ray vision and sees Taylor. He says, "There you are!!"
He puts his left hand up and gave her a wedgie without even touching her. Then he put his hand down. Taylor's wedgie went away, but she was now under Wedgie Man's control.

Jacob escaped and went to Roanoke, while Wedgie Man and Taylor went to Kevin's hideout.

"Gretchen, some guy named Wedgie Man has kidnapped my sister Taylor!" said Jacob. "Now Wedgie Man can control her every move. I don't know how to beat him. All I know is if Wedgie Man holds his hand in the air he can give you a wedgie without even touching you. When he does that you will be under his control. I don't know how you break free of the mind control!!!"

Gretchen said, "That seems like a powerful bad guy. I will go find him, you stay here."

Kevin comes out of his room and says, "Always on the move, be careful Gretchen. You remember what happened last time when you got kicked

He puts his left hand up and gave her a wedgie without even touching her.

into the laser by Taylor Stevens."

"Yea, but I'm a better fighter than I was then Kevin," she said.
"I hope you're right. I worry about you a lot," said Kevin.

Gretchen leaves to go find Wedgie Man at the hideout. She rang the doorbell, but no one came to the door. She was about to kick the door down when suddenly Taylor was behind her.

Gretchen turned around and said, "You can't win". Then Wedgie Man came out from hiding and says, "Hey Gretchen, it is you who can't win, I am too powerful for you. Get her Taylor!!"

Taylor kicks Gretchen to the ground, but Gretchen catches her kick.

Taylor does a roll over Gretchen and gives her a wedgie, but then Gretchen farts on Taylor and she lets go. Taylor passes out from the stench and Gretchen says, "That should keep her down for a while, now I will take care of you Wedgie Man!"

"I really can't wait to give you a wedgie and make you my slave," said Wedgie Man. He threw up his right hand to start the wedgie, but his head starts to hurt really badly, and he falls to the ground. Gretchen is no longer being wedgied and Taylor was no longer under Wedgie Man's control.

Taylor does a roll over Gretchen and gives her a wedgie, but then Gretchen farts on Taylor and she lets go.

Gretchen asks what happened and looked up and saw Will and Kevin. "Wedgie Man tried to give you a wedgie, but in the middle of it he looked at you and he had a thought of you dating him," said Kevin. He did not like that because he likes to do things alone, so he passed out."

"I'm glad he passed out because that will never happen," said Gretchen. "Yea," said Kevin.

Gretchen, Kevin, Will, and Taylor all go home to rest. Taylor and Jacob go back to Richmond and Wedgie Man goes to jail.

Fixing the World

BLACK HEART SNOWMAN was in a graveyard fixing a pole in the ground. He put a yellow ball in the pole and suddenly Dr. Hulk, a zombie, came up out of the ground and tried to attack him. But Black Heart told Dr. Hulk to kill Gretchen Beckner and then he teleported to his other base.

"As you wish," he said. Dr. Hulk went to the tallest tower in the world to turn everyone into zombies and kill Gretchen.

Meanwhile, at Kevin's house, Gretchen tells Kevin that she feels like something is wrong. "Kevin, we have to get to the tower. My glasses are telling me someone is climbing a tower with some kind of bottle in his hands!!"

Kevin and Gretchen go to the tower and see a zombie pouring something out of a bottle and into the tower. Gretchen makes it to the tower and shoots an arrow at it. The zombie falls off the tower, but he made it turn dark outside and he disappeared.

It was so dark outside Gretchen could not see a thing so she turned a light on from her arrow. Dr. Hulk appeared right behind her and scratches her, making her fall.

"My name is Dr. Hulk," said the zombie, "and I'm here to change the world so people know how I feel as a zombie. You will be my next zombie GRETCHEN BECKNER!!!"

"No, I will stop you and I will not give up!!" she said.
"Very well then, suit yourself," he said. As he is about to kill her, a ball

lands on his back and blows up, making him fall to the ground.

It was Kevin who threw the ball. Gretchen thanked Kevin for saving her life. "You're welcome," said Kevin.

But just then Dr. Hulk got up and says, "Kevin, you and Gretchen are so selfish-I will win!!"

Suddenly Bill comes by on a go cart and runs over Dr. Hulk's toe. "YAMATO!!!," said Dr. Hulk, as he fell into the grave that he came from. He got sealed back up in his grave forever.

"That was easy," said Gretchen!
"Yea," said Kevin.

Then Kevin and Gretchen go home to rest at Kevin's house.

Gretchen's Sister

BREEZY BECKNER, Gretchen's sister, was popular in high school, but she hated her sister. At the Beckner house, Breezy thinks about how many bad guys Gretchen has beaten and how popular she has gotten.

"I can't stand knowing that Gretchen is more popular than me," Breezy said. "I will get her back for this!!" Breezy left the house and went to Kevin's.

Meanwhile, Gretchen says "I feel like my sister is coming over- I need to talk to her."
"Ok," said Kevin.

Breezy makes it to Kevin's house and says "Gretchen, you should not be so popular, I should. I have always hated you because you think you are so cool!!"

Gretchen tries to tell Breezy that it does not matter who is the most popular, but before she could say that Breezy kicked her to the ground. She tied Gretchen's hands together and taped her mouth shut and told Kevin to stay out of this!!

"This is my fight," she said to Kevin.
"Gretchen, I will leave you here and do your job and save this world," said Breezy.

But then Red Heart Snowman shows up and says, "I heard what you said Breezy. You need to untie Gretchen and take the tape off her mouth. It does not matter who is more popular, so long as someone wins the battle in the end. But just make sure it is the hero and not the bad guy.

"You're right," said Breezy. "I'm sorry"

Breezy frees Gretchen and tells her she is sorry. Gretchen forgives her, and Red Heart says, "I know the person behind all this."

"Who?" asked Kevin.

"His name is Black Heart Snowman, the most powerful snowman ever. Kevin, we need to go stop him!" said Red Heart. "But be careful of his army men. This fight will be hard. Breezy, we will need you to help us."

"I will help," said Breezy.
"Ok, now let's get moving!" said Red Heart.
Everyone says ok and they all go to Black Heart's base!

The Big War

WHEN they got to Black Heart's base, they saw snowmen all around. Red Heart went in the base through a window and Gretchen shot an arrow at the door and blew it up.

An alarm goes off and all the snowmen surround Gretchen, Breezy, and Kevin. Kevin throws a bomb in the air, Breezy shoots it with her pistol, and it blows up all the snowmen.

Kevin and his team went into the base and saw a camera with stun darts attached to it. Gretchen shot the camera with her pistol and the camera went out, but then there was an explosion in the other room. Kevin and his team ran into the room and found Black Heart Snowman.

Red Heart was on the ground trying to recover from the bomb and said, "Kevin, step in, I need to recover from the blast!"

"Ok," said Kevin. He ran up to Black Heart, but Black Heart surrounded himself with a force field, stopping Kevin. Black Heart shot a laser beam from his heart right at Gretchen, but Breezy jumped in the way to save her.

Breezy turned into dust and Gretchen screamed, "BREEZY!!!" Gretchen started crying that her sister was dead. Black Heart says, "So sad your sister had to die. I thought she would make a good bad guy since she has always hated you."

Gretchen says, "SHUT UP!! I was bullied in high school and thought I wanted to become a bad guy too, but I didn't because I hate being

Black Heart shot a laser beam from his heart right at Gretchen, but Breezy jumped in the way to save her.

bad. It is just in my genes to be good, not bad! I will stop you no matter what happens!!"

"And just how will you do that?" asked Black Heart.
Gretchen shot her arrows at Black Heart, but he dodges all of them.
"See, you can't even hit me, how are you going to stop me?" he said.

But one of Gretchen's arrows hit the wall. The wall blew up and a red hockey stick fell on the floor and shot a beam at Black Heart, blowing him up.
"That's how!" said Gretchen.

"How did you know a hockey stick would beat him?" asked Kevin.

"Because my red glasses analyzed him to see his weakness and I discovered what it was."

"Cool!!" said Kevin.

Red Heart said, "Good job beating Black Heart Snowman everyone. Now that he is done, we can go home and rest."

"OK," said Kevin.

Gretchen says ok too but walks over to the dust. "I'm sorry you had to die Breezy, but I will finish what you started and that is defending the world, with you watching over me. Thank you for saving me. Ok, I'm ready to go Kevin."

Kevin, Gretchen, and Red Heart Snowman went back home to rest.

Gretchen says ok too but walks over to the dust.

Wedgie Death!

AT Kevin's house Kevin is nervously sitting in a chair.

"Are you okay Kevin?", asked Gretchen.
"I feel like some bad guy is going to kill us."
"Kevin I think the world is safe now I don't think you need to worry."
"I hope so," he replied.
"I know so," said Gretchen.

Kevin and Gretchen go to a party. At the party Kevin gets call from Kaitlin.
"Hello," said Kevin.
"Hey Kevin, there is a weird reading on my scanner saying that some person named Wedgie Girl is coming to kill everyone!," said Kaitlin
"Really?"
"Yes, I have been analyzing her and it looks like if she gives you a Wedgie you will die. The only way to stop her is to give her a Wedgie - that will bring the dead people back to life."
"I knew something was wrong," said Kevin. "I will tell Gretchen!"
"No, Wedgie Girl wants you and Gretchen dead. Let me handle her!"
"Are you sure?"
"Yes, I will handle it. Talk to you later," and Kaitlin

hangs up.

Kevin looks at Gretchen and asks her if she wants to play a game of chess.
"Sure."

Meanwhile Kaitlin went to the Wedgie Base and hid behind a wall! She saw an Army man talking to Wedgie Girl.
"Wedgie Girl, I can't find Gretchen and Kevin any-where," said the army man.
"Keep looking, they must be around here somewhere!"
Kaitlin runs out from behind the wall and trips the army man!
"I'm here to stop you Wedgie Girl!"
"Die Kaitlin!!" she replied.
An army of soldiers starts shooting Kaitlin! She tossed two sticky balls at the soldiers and they both get shocked and fall to the ground!

Wedgie Girl sees it and says, "That's it!!"

She pressed a button on her arm and a tank came out of nowhere!
"That's not good," thought Kaitlin.
The tank tried to shoot Kaitlin, but she jumped behind a wall! She tossed a disc at the tank, blew it up, and came out from behind the wall.

Meanwhile Kevin beat Gretchen in chess!

"Give it up Wedgie Girl," Kaitlin shouted!
"Never!!" replied Wedgie Girl.

Wedgie Girl pressed a button on the wall!
"See you around Kaitlin, I will kill you later! Hey army men, let's go to that party."

The Wedge Base started blowing up!
"I've got to get out of here," thought Kaitlin.

She ran to the door, but it was locked! Then, she saw a window and jumped, making it out of the exploding base just in time!

"That was close, but I made it. I better call Kevin," she thought.

Meanwhile Kevin beat Gretchen in chess!
"You win," Gretchen said, as the phone was ringing.

Kevin answered the phone.
"Kevin, I could not stop Wedgie Girl. She is coming to the party, you need to get out," shouted Kaitlin.
"Do I tell Gretchen about Wedgie Girl," he asked?
"Yes!"
"Ok," he says, and hangs up the phone.

"Gretchen, we must leave this party - Wedgie Girl is coming to kill us!"

"Ok, wait, who is Wedgie Girl," she asked.
"I'll tell you later, right now we have to go!"
"Why?," asked Gretchen.

At that same moment, Wedgie Girl kicks down the door and
she and the army men come in the party!
"FREEZE!" they shouted.
"Kevin, get out of my way," said Gretchen. "I need to save
these people!!"
"No Gretchen, Kaitlin has it covered!"
"No Kevin, teamwork is better than one person taking care of
this. That is what you told me, remember?" said Gretchen.
"Yeah true, but.."
"But nothing," said Gretchen!

Gretchen runs to the army men!
"GRETCHEN!!" shouted Kevin.

The army men shot at Gretchen, but she dodged all the bullets! But then Wedgie Girl appeared behind Gretchen!

"Gretchen, it's you - die!!" said Wedgie Girl.

Wedgie Girl tried to give Gretchen a wedgie, but Kaitlin
jumped in front of her and pushed her hands away!
"Kaitlin you made it out alive!!" said Gretchen.
"Yes, I did. And as for you Gretchen you should have left with
Kevin!"
"Why don't you want me to help!"
"I don't want you to die!"
"I won't Kaitlin, trust me."

Wedgie girl tried to give Gretchen a wedgie, but Kaitlin jumped in front of her and pushed her hands away!

"Out of my way Kaitlin, I want Gretchen!" shouted Wedgie Girl.

But then someone tripped her. "Who tripped me," asked Wedgie Girl.

Joey comes out of a corner of the wall and says, "It's me, Joey. I tripped you!"
"Kaitlin, Kevin told us all about team work and how you won't let Gretchen help. We can easily kick you off the team if you don't want to work together."
"Right, sorry, go head Gretchen."
"Thank you," said Gretchen.

Wedgie Girl gets up from the ground and says, "Looks like I'm out numbered, but who cares, I will still win! Men, stay back I've got this!"

Kevin enters the party room again.
"Guys, as part of a team, let Gretchen handle this fight. If something goes wrong we can step in. I want to see if Gretchen has gotten stronger!"
"Are you sure," asked Kaitlin?
"Yes, I'm positive."
"Ok," Joey and Kaitlin answer in unison.
"Thank you Kevin," said Gretchen.

Gretchen swings her swords at Wedgie Girl, but she jumps out of the way.

"You're way to slow Gretchen," shouted Wedgie Girl.
"Really, are you sure," asked Gretchen?

Gretchen kicks Wedgie Girl in midair and she falls
to the ground.
"I win!" said Gretchen

Just then the police show up, pointing their guns at
Wedgie Girl. "FREEZE, you're under arrest!" they
shout.

Wedgie Girl puts her hands in the air and all the
army men drop their guns.

"We surrender," they say.
Kevin says, "Ok, you army men are free to go."

The army men leave and Wedgie Girl goes to jail.
Joey, Kaitlin, Kevin, Gretchen go home!

In jail, Wedgie Man is crying. "I want to date Gretch-
en so bad but I can't I'm a bad guy," he said.

Wedgie Girl replies, "I kind of like Gretchen too
Wedgie Man, but she is nothing like us. We are bad
guys and isn't being bad more fun than worrying
about stupid Gretchen Beckner?!"
"You're right," said Wedgie Man, "When we get out
of here we will finally get rid of Gretchen Beckner!"
"There you go," Wedgie Girl replied

"My old team was, Kaitlin, Emily, Dominic, Robbie and me. We were sword fighting a guy named Fake Kevin, who had the power to separate us. After our separation, it was just you and me plus Dominic, Kaitlin, and Joey! But in the end, I ended up beating the Fake Kevin robot

The Army!

AT the army hide out, a guy named J.J.(the mad-
man that created an evil Fake Kevin robot) was
ordering the army to destroy Kevin's team!
J.J yelled, "Team, destroy Kevin's team for blowing
up my fake Kevin"!
All the army men responded, "YES SIR!!"

J.J. goes to find Kevin's team! Meanwhile Kevin
was talking to Gretchen about his old team!

"My old team was, Kaitlin, Emily, Dominic, Rob-
bie and me. We were sword fighting a guy named
Fake Kevin, who had the power to separate us.
After our separation, it was just you and me plus
Dominic, Kaitlin, and Joey! But in the end, I ended
up beating the Fake Kevin robot!"
"I bet that was hard to do," said Gretchen.
"Yes, it was," replied Kevin.

Kevin and Gretchen heard an explosion outside!
They raced outside to see what it was.

"FREEZE, WITH YOUR HANDS IN THE AIR!!"
shouted the army soldier.

Kevin and Gretchen put their hands in the air.
"What's happening and what was that explosion?"
asked Gretchen.
The soldier replied, "The explosion was J.J. blowing
up the doors. He is trying to find all the members of
Kevin's team so he can destroy them! You're coming
with us to J.J.'s base."
"You won't get away with this," said Kevin.
"Less talking and more moving," replied the soldier.

The army soldiers bring Kevin and Gretchen to J.J.
"J.J., I've got the leader of Kevin's team," said the sol-
dier to J.J.
"Good," said J.J. "Go put Gretchen in the death room
and Kevin in jail!
"YES SIR!" the soldier replied.

The army soldiers tossed Gretchen in the death room
and took Kevin to the jail.

"I have to get out of here and save Gretchen," thought
Kevin. "But I need the key."

Kevin sees the key laying on the table outside of the
jail cell and wonders how he is going to reach it.

Meanwhile, Gretchen is thinking about how she is
going to find Kevin.

J.J. enters the room and says, "You will die here Gretch-en!"

He presses a button that takes the oxygen out of the room.

"I can't breathe!!" gasps Gretchen, and she
falls to the ground!!
"HA! HA!! HA!!! goodbye Gretchen," laughs J.J.

"No," thought Gretchen, "I can't let the bad guy win!!"

But when it seemed that Gretchen was about to die, Joey
shot the jail cell with his machine gun, which opened
Gretchen's cell and lets the oxygen quickly came back on.

"What? Who saved me?" asked Gretchen.
"You're safe with me now Gretchen, now let's go save
Kevin and stop J.J.," said Joey.
"Thank you Joey!"
"You're welcome Gretchen!"

Meanwhile Kevin is still working on the key.
"I can't get the key, but I wonder if I can hack the jail
cell?" he thought.
He tries hacking the cell and it works! The door to the
cell opens.

"HEY! Get back in your cell," shouts the soldier.

"Hey, want to play catch?" asks Kevin?
He tossed a ball at the soldier, shocking him, and making him fall on the ground.

"Now to find Gretchen," he shouted.
He didn't see that Joey and Gretchen were behind him.
"Kevin, it's me Joey. I saved Gretchen and now we need to stop J.J.!"

Kevin turned around. "I know, thanks for your help," he said.

Kevin, Joey, and Gretchen run outside to find J.J.

"There he is, he's leaving the base," yelled Joey!
"We will never make it to him," said Kevin.
"Yes, we will," said Gretchen. "Stay here, I've got this. If I don't come back then come help me!"

"Oh, trust me I will," replied Kevin.

Gretchen runs to her motorcycle and chases after J.J. She jumps on top of him, but he pushes her off and he takes out a machine gun!

"I would love to see you get past this big gun," he yells!

He shoots the gun at Gretchen but she dodges all the bullets!!

"Give up J.J., she yells!

Suddenly an army solider comes up from behind and tases

Gretchen.

"Give up Gretchen," yells J.J.!

"Never!," she shouts back, slowly getting up.

But then Joey jumps out of the window, shoots the soldier and J.J., and they both go down.

"Get up J.J., get up," shouted Joey!

J.J. gets up and says, "What are you going to do, kill me?"

Just then Kevin comes out of the door and says, "It's over J.J., you're surrounded by the police."

"You're going to jail J.J.," said one of the cops. "For building a Fake Kevin and trying to kill people!"

"Kevin, it was you that called the cops," said J.J.

"Yes, I did."

"I will be back," said J.J. "Just you wait!"

"Yeah right," said Joey.

The police take J.J. off to jail.

Joey says to Kevin, "I've got to go talk to my brother Will, I'll see you later."

"Ok," says Kevin.

Kevin turns to Gretchen and says, "I feel like something is wrong."

"What's wrong," she says.

"I don't know," says Kevin. "Let's go back to the house and rest, maybe that's all I need."

"Sounds good," said Gretchen, "it's been a long day!"

Kevin and Gretchen go rest!

THE END!

CPSIA information can be obtained
at www.ICGtesting.com
Printed in the USA
BVHW021140220820
586465BV00023B/229